Jet, the Little Robot

Story by Annette Smith

Illustrations by Richard Hoit

Harry and Mom
went into a big store.

"I am going to look
at the robots," said Harry.

Harry looked for a little robot in a red box.

"I cannot see the little robot,"

said Harry.

"He is not here."

Harry looked and looked
for the little robot.

"Where are you, Little Robot?"
said Harry.

"Where are you?"

Click! Click! Click!

Harry looked up.

"I can see you, Little Robot,"

he said.

"Mom! Mom!" shouted Harry.

"Look!

The little robot is up **here**."

"Here you are, Harry,"

said Mom.

"Jet, the Little Robot,

is for you."

Click! Click! Click!